Old Saybrook, CT 06475

W9-AMQ-599

DATE DUE

Adapted by Lee Howard
Illustrated by Alcadia Snc
Based on the episode "A Scooby-Doo Christmas" by John Collier,
George Doty IV, Jim Krieg, and Ed Scharlach

WWW.ABDOPUBLISHING.COM

Reinforced library bound edition published in 2015 by Spotlight, a division of ABDO
PO Box 398166, Minneapolis, Minnesota 55439.
Spotlight produces high-quality reinforced library bound editions for schools and libraries.
Published by agreement with Warner Bros. Entertainment Inc.

Printed in the United States of America, North Mankato, Minnesota.
052014   072014

 THIS BOOK CONTAINS
RECYCLED MATERIALS

LIBRARY OF CONGRESS CATALOGING-IN-PUBLICATION DATA

Howard, Lee.
  Scooby-doo comic storybook / adapted by Lee Howard ; art by Alcadia Snc. -- Reinforced library bound ed.
    pages cm
  Four graphic novels, previously published separately.
  ISBN 978-1-61479-281-9 (#1: A haunted Halloween) -- ISBN 978-1-61479-282-6 (#2: A merry scary holiday) -- ISBN 978-1-61479-283-3 (#3:
Camp Fear) -- ISBN 978-1-61479-284-0 (#4: Dino destruction)
  1. Graphic novels. I. Howard, Lee. Haunted Halloween. II. Howard, Lee. Merry scary holiday. III. Howard, Lee. Camp fear. IV. Howard, Lee. Dino
destruction. V. Alcadia (Firm) VI. Scooby-Doo (Television program) VII. Title.
  PZ7.7.H74Sco 2015
  741.5'973--dc23
                    2014005381

'Tis the night before Christmas, and Scooby and the kids from Mystery, Inc. are heading to Daphne's uncle's house in Mills Corner.

The Mystery Machine skids to the side of the icy road, knocking over the presents inside the van.

The gang scrambles outside to check on the Mystery Machine. That's when they hear loud screams.

JEEPERS! I WONDER WHAT THAT WAS ALL ABOUT.

CREEPY SNOWMAN! LIKE, RUN FOR YOUR LIVES!

The gang escapes from the snowman — and crash-lands in front of the town inn.

YOU'D BEST LEAVE WINTER HOLLOW. THERE'S NO CHRISTMAS HERE, THANKS TO THE SNOW MONSTER!

CRASH!

There's a loud noise from the street outside. The gang runs outside to investigate.

THE SNOW MONSTER DESTROYED MY CHIMNEY! HOW IS SANTA GOING TO COME NOW?

A little boy explains that he was waiting at home for Santa when the snow monster wrecked his chimney.

IT'S TIME TO CATCH THAT SNOWMAN. LET'S FOLLOW HIS TRACKS!

It isn't long before the gang finds what they're looking for.

ZOINKS!

RUN!

Fred, Daphne, Velma, Shaggy, and Scooby hide in an old shed.

SORRY, MAN. LIKE, OCCUPIED!

BRRR!

The snowman picks up the shed and throws it!

Back at the inn . . .

HMMM . . . THAT SNOW MONSTER KEEPS DESTROYING CHIMNEYS, AND THAT SURE HAS HELPED BUSINESS HERE AT THE INN.

THIS IS PROFESSOR HIGGENSON. HE WROTE A BOOK ABOUT THE SNOW MONSTER. MAYBE HE CAN HELP.

THE SNOW MONSTER IS THE GHOST OF BLACKJACK BRODY. LONG AGO, BRODY STOLE GOLD FROM SEAMUS FAGIN.

Velma reads from the professor's book.

IT SAYS HERE THAT BRODY GOT AWAY. ACCORDING TO LEGEND, HE WAS FROZEN INSIDE A SNOWMAN, AND THE STOLEN GOLD WAS NEVER FOUND.

Blackjack Brody

The gang heads outside to do a little more investigating.

THAT SNOWMAN COMES BACK EVERY CHRISTMAS TO LOOK FOR THE GOLD. HE TARGETS THE OLDEST HOUSES IN TOWN. I BET HE LOOKS IN JEB'S HOUSE NEXT!

LET'S CHECK IT OUT!

Scooby and the kids peek into Jeb's house. Guess who's coming to Christmas dinner!

JEEPERS!

The gang hides, then follows the snow monster back outside.

Fred, Daphne, and Velma throw snowballs at the snow monster, chasing it toward the ice . . .

But the snow monster's loud roar starts a deep crack across the ice.

Daphne and Velma help Scooby and Shaggy warm up.

The gang heads back to the inn to plan their next move.

I WONDER ABOUT THAT SHERIFF.

WHAT ABOUT THE INNKEEPER? HE'S GETTING RICH EVERY WINTER.

As Shaggy and Scooby sit by the fireplace, an icy draft blows down the chimney. The fire goes out, and the room grows cold.

UH-OH, SCOOB.
HE'S BACK!

In the dark, Shaggy and Scooby stumble into a box of Christmas lights.

The two buddies run up the stairs and out onto the rooftop. They need to find a way down, fast.

Fred has a plan to melt the snowman —
the town's heat lamps!

Daphne hits a
switch, and all
the heat lamps
turn on at once.

OH, NO!
I'M MELTING!

24

There's a strange machine inside the snowman.

Velma pushes a red button on the machine. It opens up to reveal . . .

PROFESSOR HIGGENSON!

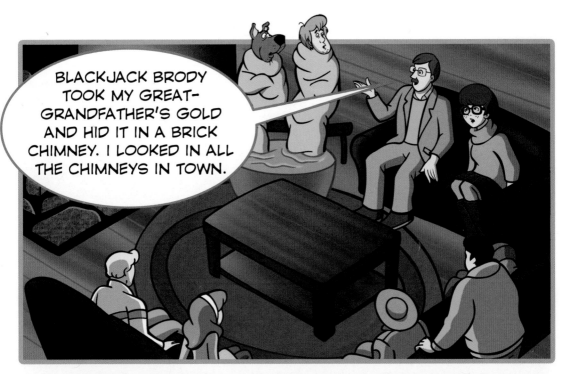

BLACKJACK BRODY TOOK MY GREAT-GRANDFATHER'S GOLD AND HID IT IN A BRICK CHIMNEY. I LOOKED IN ALL THE CHIMNEYS IN TOWN.

BUT ALL I FOUND WERE BRICKS.

Velma picks up a brick from the broken chimney and wipes away the soot. The brick is made of pure gold!